SCOTT COUNTY LIBRARY
SHAKOPEE, MN 55379

STARS

Elisa Peters

PowerKiDS press
New York

Published in 2013 by The Rosen Publishing Group, Inc.
29 East 21st Street, New York, NY 10010

Copyright © 2013 by The Rosen Publishing Group, Inc.

All rights reserved. No part of this book may be reproduced in any form without permission in writing from the publisher, except by a reviewer.

First Edition

Editor: Amelie von Zumbusch
Book Design: Kate Laczynski

Photo Credits: Cover Pat Gaines/Flickr/Getty Images; pp. 4, 8, 10, 12, 16, 20, 22, 24 (galaxy, stars) Shutterstock.com; p. 6 Stuart O'Sullivan/Stone/Getty Images; p. 14 Comstock/Comstock/Thinkstock; p. 18 iStockphoto/Thinkstock

Library of Congress Cataloging-in-Publication Data

Peters, Elisa.
 Stars / by Elisa Peters. — 1st ed.
  p. cm. — (Powerkids readers: the Universe)
 Includes index.
 ISBN 978-1-4488-7388-3 (library binding) — ISBN 978-1-4488-7534-4 (pbk.) — ISBN 978-1-4488-7540-5 (6-pack)
 1. Stars—Juvenile literature. I. Title.
 QB801.7.P45 2013
 523.8—dc23

2011048267

Manufactured in the United States of America

CPSIA Compliance Information: Batch #CS12PK: For Further Information contact Rosen Publishing, New York, New York at 1-800-237-9932

CONTENTS

Stars   5
The Sun   15
The Milky Way   21
Words to Know   24
Index   24
Websites   24

There are many **stars**.

Stars are made of gas.

Blue stars are the hottest stars.

10

Stars beam out heat and light.

Light travels very fast.

14

The **Sun** is a star.

It keeps Earth warm.

Earth circles the Sun.

The Sun is in the Milky Way **galaxy**.

Galaxies have many stars.

WORDS TO KNOW

galaxy

stars

Sun

INDEX

E
Earth, 17, 19

G
galaxy, 21, 23

H
heat, 11

L
light, 11, 13

WEBSITES

Due to the changing nature of Internet links, PowerKids Press has developed an online list of websites related to the subject of this book. This site is updated regularly. Please use this link to access the list: www.powerkidslinks.com/pkrtu/stars/